Mochtar Lubis'
The Angus Monster Collection
I

In Memory of
Mochtar Lubis
1922-2004

Chapter 1: New Beginning

So In July 1977, The Tanners Lived In The Los Angeles, California. Kate, Willie and Lynn Lived In Their House, They Had a Pet Cat Named Lucky, So Lynn Enjoyed Cleaning Up Her Dishes, Kate Was Noticing To Her Daughter, Lynn Said "Hi, Kate", Unfortunately Kate Said To Lynn "Hi Lynn, How's Your Doing?",

She Continues To Clean Her Dishes By Excitement, She Became a Happiness Owned By Her Father Willie, He Said To Lynn "Hi Lynn, How Are You Doing Over There?", Lynn Said "I Was Cleaning My Dishes In The Kitchen",

Just a Been At The Time as Lynn Snuffled Up Her Nose as Her Human Kind, She Caught a Smell An Alien Scent, It Was Angus Monster, Possibly He Did Know To Lynn Tanner, That Happened.... Angus Monster Said "Hey Lynn, Why Did You Clean Your Dishes?",

Willie Walked In and Told Angus Monster When Asked "How Did You Get There?", Angus Monster Said Back "I Was Here", Kate Waited and Waited and Waited, She Said "I Know Right" as She Got Up "I Knew That Happened To You, Angus", Kate Understand About Angus' Life, Then She Cleaned Up Her Living Room Immediately.

Lynn Had Known To Angus' Kindness, She Knew For Him, She Has To Know About The Hagen Family, Lynn Said "We Need To Know About The Hagens To See How We Take The Lead By The Hagen Family".

Probably, Lynn Sniffed The Several Weeks Between The Smell and The Aroma, Besides She Needed To See How Angus' Job Like Over Hanging Out With The Hagen Family, Something Happened When Willie Said To Lynn "Okay, We Cannot Go Without Kate Tanner", Meanwhile Kate Finished Cleaning The Living Room, She Decided To Say To Her Husband Willie Tanner "I Notice About You Forgetting Me", After That.

Lynn Tanner Knew Wanted Angus Monster To Take The Lead With The Hagen Family Which They Had a Horse Carriage With The Brown Horse Named Harry, Willie and Kate Also Takes Them The Lead Too, Kate Said "Okay Lynn, Our Journey Begins".

Then, They Met The Hagen Family, The Adult Boy Named Daniel That Has His Father, Wallace and His Wife Madia, They Had No Wait To Go To The Farm.

Angus Monster Said "Okay Lynn, Show Me How I Am an Alien Dog Monster That Blasted Me as a Melmacian Dog Like Creature".

Lynn Said Back To Angus Monster "I Believe You Angus, Just Trust Me as You Can".

Then, They Got Into The Fitting Seat of Horse Carriage, The Hagen Family Knows For Something New, Wallace Led Angus and The Tanners To The Old Farm With That Son Daniel and His Mother Madia.
 Sometimes Later, They Got Into The Old Farm To See The Animals, Something Knows To Get Better For Helping Others, They Imagined First Time.

Kate and Willie Went To The Farm, They Didn't Promise For Happening, Everything Didn't Get Right For Them, Willie Said "I Feel Too Sacramento For Me When I Didn't See That Coming", Mostly When Kate Promised Willie "I'm Sure It Is Promising Way To Do With, Willie".

Kate Knew That Angus Monster Cannot Stop Eating Cats, The Quite For Planet Dave's Which Angus' Life and Promising For Willows, Maybe He is a Cat Eater, Angus Said "I'm a Cat Eater from Plant Dave", Suddenly All The Sudden, Lynn Tanner Was Very Peace and Quiet and Nice.

It Happened, She's Nice To The Cows and Nice Pigs, She Promised For Farm Animals, She Said "I Know About The Farm Which It is Very Old".
Sometimes She Would a Been To See The Cows, Lynn Said To The Cows "I'm Sure Cows Are The Most Precious Animal".

Noticing Where Angus Monster's Delightful Ways To Say To The Others, Lynn Didn't Know About The Farm, Sometimes She Can't Afford for Something Else.

Lynn Said To The Pigs "I Like Noticing About Bacon and Departed Something Else as Well" She Thinks For Someone Going on in the Farm "I Knew How It is, Willie".

As She is Going to Ask With Her Father Willie Tanner, As Angus Monster Sees Something In The Farm,

By Something Which Kate Had Something New.

As It Suffers for Something, Kate Watched The Good White Clouds Moving Away from the Blue Sky, Purportedly Kate Said "Beside What Clouds Are Moving Down The Below", She Didn't Know For Some Kind of Sheep.

Sometimes Madia Used The Rake. She Said "You Know I Am Doing Here, Kate".

She Believed First as She Did Like Rest of the Tanners, Wallace Hagen Knows For Someone Else's Plates, He Has Been Caught The Plates For The Family, He Said "I Know For Dinner Mercy For Lunch at All, Madia" as He Puts The Plates Into The Picnic Carpet.

Daniel Noticed The Kindness or Happiness, He Could Put The Glass of Cups on The Picnic Too, He Just Talk To His Father Wallace.

Daniel Said "I Can't Understand How He Didn't Find The Troops, Wallace".
Then, Angus Monster Met The Hagen Family, He Said To Them "I Understand How I Came Here, The Hagen Family".

Madia Know About The Alien, She Said To Angus "I Know How He Is!"

Then Wallace Said To Him "Oh Wow! He Has a Brown-Green Fur, He is a Shaped Like Melmacian But Melmacian-Like Dog Creature, Has a Same Tail and Has a Fluffiest Hair That He Has!".

Sometimes, Angus Knows How He Can Survive The Fight of the Fires or He Has No Idea That He Is. Wallace Said "I Need Something To Get Comfortable and We Want Them To Go Back To The House Real Soon".

Even Angus Monster Thinks Wallace Mentioned The Sheeps Sometimes With His Wife, Only The Sheep Makes a Noise After Angus' Problems.

Willie Had a Problem With His Daughter Lynn Tanner, Someday Where Kate Told Lynn How To See The Animals as Well.

Willie and Lynn Were Both Talking In Conversation Purposely, "I Know How He Can Get Strong as Melmacians" Said Willie "I Know It For a Plan, Lynn".

Angus Monster Heard The Message On Willie Tanner's Sight, He Sees Anything But The Hagen Family,

Wallace Said "I Knew He's Quiet and Peaceful".

Peacefully When Angus Monster Becomes Too Tired and Sweet, He Didn't Get Anything To Sleep All Night as Well.

Possibly Angus Didn't Notice For Someone Still Going On The Picnic Without Him, He Knows First But First, Wallace Said To Madia "I Wanna Know How I Am Saving My Life Before Late Than Never, Miss".

He Doesn't Know For All For Madia's Fair, Madia Said To Wallace "We Should Do Something To Eat".

They Got No Attitude for Doing Something But Angus Monster Thought For Food To Eat All The Time,

He Said "I Have No Idea What Is, Madia".

As Later, Angus and The Tanners Got Back Home.

Chapter 2: The Conditioning

So, Angus Monster Saw Lucky Tanner Sitting on The Old Time Chair, Angus Monster Said "I'm Going To Eat Lucky Tanner as of Yet".

All The Sudden, He Started To Chase Lucky Off The Chair, Angus Gets Into The Kitchen To Chase Lucky Away from Him, as Lucky Yowls at Him.

Meanwhile, Willie Tanner Woke Up To The Angus Monster Chasing The Family Pet Cat Lucky, He Got Into The Kitchen.

He Told Angus Monster To Say "You Shouldn't Eat Cats In The House!".

Suddenly, Kate and Lynn Woke Up To Speak Up To Willie and Angus, Lynn Said "I Know How They Didn't See That, Willie".

Sometimes Kate Spoke To Lynn "I Knew How That Happened, Lynn" Kate Picked Up The Dishes Immediately "I Suppose To Clean The Dishes as Well and! I Need To Do The Dinnertime For Tonight".

Unfortunately, Lynn Tanner Saw Something Out of There, She Said "Okay, Kate".

Then, She Walks To The Living Room To Watch The Television Show, She Relaxed On The Chair For Days, Angus Monster Doesn't Give Up To Lucky's Life.

Lucky Took Over The Lifeless Into The Couch To See Lynn's Fractional Life From Watching The Cartoons, He Did To Her.

Angus Monster Saw Lucky Sitting on The Couch, Kate Arrived and Spoke Up To Lynn from The Charity That Lucky is on the Couch.

Kate Asked "What is That?!".

Lynn Answered "It's Lucky Sitting on the Couch".

Angus' Charity Was Spoke Up By Lynn.

"I Knew For My Life at All When My Cat is on Our Couch" Said Lynn Tanner.

"Mostly, I Don't Know for Further Notice" Said Angus Monster "I Knew What Happened For Me The End of Asking Myself"

Suddenly, He Sees Lucky On The Couch, Which He Came Up In The Living Room.

Willie Came Up and Yelled at Lucky "Get Lucky Off My Couch!".

Then, Lucky Ran Away from The Couch, Willie Got a Scam for Angus Monster's Mystery.

The Next Day, Kate and Lynn Were Discovering In The Backyard To See However They Done as Well. Lynn Said "I Wonder How The Rabbit Is".

"I'm Impressed How You Are Great" Said Kate "I Knew How It Happens".
Suddenly, Kate and Lynn Looked Down The Ground, They Saw a Dead Rabbit Who Possibly Died from Poisoning.

"What was That?" Asked Kate.

"It's a Dead Rabbit, Kate" Said Lynn "I Wonder Know Why They Died Unfortunately Due To The Massive Poisoning from The Backyards".

All The Sudden, Lynn and Kate Walked To The Front Yard Seeing The Flowers Blooming Outside the House, But Angus Monster Started To Disappear from The House.

From The Distance, Angus Monster Can't See Anything From The Sun, Sometimes Lynn Stopped From The Distance.

Lynn Yelled "Hey! Come Back Here!".

But Angus Monster Got Back In The House Shortly After Being Yelled By His Best Friend, Lynn Tanner as of Yet.

One Night, The Wind Came Up The Storm, The Living Was Very Quiet, Angus Monster Was Asleep on The Kate's Chair, He Snored Loudly as Lucky Can't Afford Something To Eat All The Cat Food Unfortunately.

Suddenly, Lynn Tanner Wanted Angus Monster To Wake Up "Angus, Wake Up!" She Grunted Against The Sleeping Alien "Wake Up, Please Wake Up".

She Knows That Angus Monster Can't Wake Which He Is Very Tired and Sleepy All The Time, Lynn Just Rushed To Her Parents' Bedroom And Then Kate To See How The Pet Alien is Still Asleep.

Kate Asked "Lynn, What's Going On?"

Lynn Answered To Kate "Angus Monster is Still Asleep".

Then Lucky Tanner, A Cat Went Arrived To Kate's Control, So Kate Knew That is To See How It is a Family Pet Cat.

Lynn Said "That's Lucky, My Family Pet Cat" She Noticed To Kate "That's How He Lived".

Lynn Knows She Has To Do Something With Angus Monster, Just a Shut for Something as Lynn Said "I Notice, He Has To Do Something Like That, Kate".

Sometimes, Lynn Tanner Knew That She is Been Told By Her Father Willie Tanner.
Willie Then Said "Okay, Angus Needs To Wake Up from The Difference".

Mostly Lynn Knows The Answers For Her Father as That Day.

All The Sudden, Kate Picked Up Lucky as of Going Back To The Living Room, Being a Distance Between Lynn and Willie as If Knowing.

Kate Wished She Could Wake Angus Monster Up For The Time of Awakening.

But Willie Knows The Questions, Lynn Coughed a Little Bit and Groaned, She Scratched Her Arm as She Thinks of an Awakening for Angus Monster's Ability But He Does Go To Sleep A Lot.

Knowing When The Tanners was Before Kate Got Pregnant.

Chapter 3: The Hagen Wanted

So The Next Morning, The Hunter Recently Coming Up To The Hagen's Backyard.

So, Daniel, Wallace and Madia Were Asleep in the Bedroom Alone, Mostly It Happened When Harry The Horse Starts Eating Grass in the Backyard Eventually.

The Hunter Got Mad, He's Holding His Gun Immediately as He Gets a Temper Hunting, Unfortunately The Hagens Woke Up To See That The Brown Horse Harry Was Still Eating Grass.

But The Hunter Grabbed The Gun, Pulling The Trigger as He Gets Angry. Madia Yelled at The Window Loudly "Hunter, Don't!".

and Then, The Hunter Actually Shoots The Horse, Definitely It Was Harry, He Got Shot In The Chest, Collapsed and Possibly Dies.

Unfortunately Madia is Just Walling Over The Death of Harry, She Cried "My Poor Old Horse!".

She, Wallace and Daniel Got Out The Door of the House, Rushed To The Harry's Dead Body as They Mourn Over Him.

Wallace Cried Loudly "What Happened To My Harry! I Don't Know Why He's Already Gone!".

He Sniffled To Sob Away from The Tears Between Crying Daniel and His Mother, The Hunter Just Walked Away from Them.

All The Sudden, Daniel Sobbed Loudly in Trauma as Madia Hugged Him.

The Panic Appeared In The Rain as Wallace Hagen Started To Know What Happened To His Own Horse, He is Just Upset, He Said "I Tried To Notice But Nope. He Just Died".

Madia Just Said To Wallace "We Will Bury Him This Afternoon".

Wallace Nodded His Head Sadly as He Groaned In The Sadness Agony, He is Known to Be Upset and Depressed of Becoming Temperature.

He Saw The Clouds Moving By, The Sad Rains of the Skies Come By, as Daniel, Madia and Wallace Had Never Been Happy About The Death of the Horse.

Something Happened From Across the Skies, Daniel Realized He Missed Harry as Much as Well, Seeing By The Rainbow of The Clouds and Skies.

He Forget To Be Doing The Leading Over The Heaven of the Horse, Taking The Realize For The Sun's Announcement.

Wallace Sadly Thinks For Harry's Passing, Madia Hagen Sobbed Loudly and Sadly Over His Body, Daniel Thought For Sure as He Found The Tissue For The Tears.

The Next Day This Afternoon, Wallace Dugged Up In Front of the House, He Actually Buries Harry The Horse To The Memorial Grave.

Possibly, Daniel and Madia Watched as Wallace is Burying Him, Might of The Saddest Nightmares of All The Horses' Leads.

Daniel Sadly Comments "I Wonder Know Why How Did Harry Die?". Madia Replied To Daniel "From Gunshot Wounds, Daniel".

Sometimes, Wallace is Still Digging and Burying His Own Horse, Madia Should A Been No Seen for The Wounds of The Hunters.

"I Don't Believe What Happened To That Horse?" Asked Wallace.

"Wallace, I Know He Got Shot By The Mean Hunter By His Own" Replied Madia.

Wallace Never Knew How He Finished Burying The Horse, He is Very Sad and Depressing for Due To The Lack of Sadness.

Daniel Patted on His Father's Shoulder, Madia Knows For The Burial of the Graves, Memorial Moments To Harry's Soul.

Eventually, Wallace, Daniel and Madia Were Mourning Over The Death Sensations.

Later at Lunchtime, The Breezy Day In The Tanner's Living Room, Angus Monster Just Finally Woke Up, He Knows When It's Lunch Time.

His Caused Trouble, As He Noticed That Lucky is on The Dining Table Licking His Paw. Angus Said "I'm Just Going To Eat The Cat".

Angus Monster Unfortunately Got Up, Growled Over, Ran Up There and Chased Lucky Again, Lucky's Yowl as He is Scared of Him.

Eventually or What Things, Lynn Tanner Walked Up On Her Way Home, She Saw Angus Monster Still Chasing Lucky as of Yet.

"Uh Oh!" Cried Lynn Tanner.

Lynn Got Scared and Shocked as She Turned Out For Her Fear.

as Kate and Willie Watching The Game Show, Lynn Rushed To Her Parents.

"What's Going On In Here?" Asked Lynn.

Sometimes, Willie Looked Up and Said "I Think.... Angus Monster is Still Chasing My Cat".

Then Kate Said "I Know Right, He is Just an Alien Dog Monster".

Suddenly, Angus Monster Got Up from Seeing Lucky Walking Away from The Couch, Angus Said To Lynn "Does It Know How It Lived?".

Lynn Said To Angus "I Wonder How Something is Gotten Into That Thing".

Angus Asked To Lynn "Are You Sure It is Accepting Type?"

Lynn Answered "Yes".

So, Angus Got Into The Living Room Window as He Sees Many Hunters Coming By The Street. Angus Yelled "It's The Hunters!".

Kate Looks Shocked and Scared "Oh No! The Hunters! We Better Hide!".

Next Evening For Several Days, Willie Got To The Hagen's House, He Wonder To Ask The Hagen Family, Wallace, Daniel and Madia Looked Upset For Something.

"What's Wrong?" Asked Willie Tanner.

"I Know, My Horse Died" Cried Wallace.

"Me Too, I Wonder Why" Madia Sobbed Unfortunately.

Daniel Just Unfortunately Said "I Know Right, He's My Favorite Horse".

So, The Hagens Cry as They Mourn Over The Death of Harry, Sometimes Willie Tanner Has Comfort The Hagens.

Willie Said To The Hagen Family "Don't Worry Friends, We Will Get A New Horse".

Wallace Thinks For The Disseverment "I Wanted a Black Horse Please?"

Then, Willie Answered "Yes, Wallace, Yes, Sir".

Possibly, Madia, Daniel and Wallace Changed Their Minds For Finding a New Horse For The Farm Rescue.

Madia Cried "Yes! I'm Excited!". Daniel Nodded His Head "Me Too".

So, The Hagens Are Always Getting a New Horse For The Way, Then Willie Tanner Waved Goodbye and He Got Back To The Tanner's House as He Could Get a Dinnertime for Tonight.

Chapter 4: The Fire!

So in 1978, After The Hagen Family Brought a Black Horse Which They Call Him Harry II, For All The Sudden, Angus Monster and The Tanner Family is Now Finally Led By Wallace, Madia and Daniel To Go Back To The Old Farm.

Wallace Said "Now Lead To The Farm, Madia".

So, They Got Into The Horse Carriage For The Ride, They Always Now Went To The Old Farm, The Brown Dog Came Up For The Life of the Canine.

"I See You, Mister Dog" Said Angus Monster "I Wonder You Like Your Meal".

Angus Monster Sees The Brown Dog In The Willowing Way, He Saw a Fat Pig Playing In The Mud and The Other Pigs Eating In the Barn.

"Hey, Check This Out" Angus Said "I Knew What's Gonna Happened With Torches".

Unfortunately, The Brown Dog Saw The Pig Immediately, Then He Ran Off The Fence, Fierce Barks Was Heard on Angus' Mind.

"Hey! Come Back Here!" Yelled Angus Monster "I'm Coming After You!". The Tanner Saw The Dog Running Away from The Farm.

Lynn Said "That's The Dog, Kate, It's A Dog".

Kate Said To Lynn "I Agree, Run After Him".

The Tanners Started Running To The Brown Dog, The Hagens and Angus Monster Came Up To Chase The Dog.

The Torch Who is Lit Up The Fire, It Collapsed Around Into The Barn, The Farm Animals Were In Panicked as The Tanners, The Hagens and Angus Monster Still Chasing The Brown Dog.

Sometimes, The Fire Lights Up The Barn as It Starts, The Brown Dog Yelped as He Ran Back Off The Fence as He Got Led By The Others.

Kate and Lynn Started To Yell "FIIIRRREEEEE!!!!".

So, The Animals Started To Burn Which The Cows, Pigs, Sheeps, Ducks, Egrets, Geeses, Gooses, Chickens and Many Other Animals Dying of Melting With Fire and The Burning Intense.

The Brown Dog, Angus Monster, The Tanners and The Hagen Family Were Rushed To The Horse Carriage.

Willie Shouted "Everyone, Let's Get Out Here!".

Wallace, Daniel and Madia Have To Ride The Horse Carriage Again With The Black Male Horse, But The Hunter Just Arrives from The Brown Dog's Rush for Judgement Plurality.

Lynn Yelled "Hunter! No!".

The Hunter Grabbed The Gun, Pulls The Trigger, Shoots and Injures The Brown Dog, Kate Tanner Recently Rescues Him from Getting Shot By.

The Brown Dog Began To Whimper Loudly as Angus Monster Watched Carefully and Sadly. He Sadly Comments To The Brown Dog "I Knew What Happened To You?".

So, Kate Notices The Brown Dog That Was Injured "It's Gonna Be Okay, Buddy" So, She Spoke To The Dog "It's Okay".

So, They Got Back To The Tanner's House To Leave Automatically. Wallace Said "Take Care of Yourself, Angus and The Tanners".

As Angus Monster and The Tanners Got Out of The Horse Carriage's Backseat, The Carriage Leaves Away from The Flows of the Road.

So, Willie Cried Out of Sadness "We Missed Our Farm So Much". Angus Monster Comments Sadly "Where Are The Animals?!".

Suddenly Lynn Sadly Replies To Angus Monster "It's Okay Angus, No One Cared About Dying of The Fire".

So, Angus Monster and The Tanners Got Back Inside The House as They Needed Some Rest and Having Fun.

Chapter 5: The Dinner Joke

Meanwhile, It is Breezy Day as Angus Monster Seemly Gets To Sleep on The Chair But He Snuck To Lucky Being on The Couch, He Sniffed Over The Scent.

Willie Tanner Shows Up, Angus Monster Looked Shocked, Then It Happened. Willie Yelled "Get Lucky Off My Couch!"

Then, Lucky Jumped and Ran Out The Couch, Shortly When Kate and Lynn Walked to The Distance of The Living Room.

Willie Asked To Kate and Lynn "How Did Lucky Get Into My Couch?".

Kate Said To Willie as Eventually of Telling "Angus Did It To Him".

Totally Happened, Lynn Tanner Thinks About Something "I Know, The Cartoon is On".

Angus Monster Started Watching The Merrie Melodies Cartoon, He Said To The TV "I Loved Watching Cartoons".

So, Lynn Joins and Sits Quietly as She and Angus Began To Watch The Cartoon on Old Television as Kate and Willie Looked After The Window Getting Cold Outside.

Kate Said "It's Getting Cold Out There, There's No Need To Go Outside Forever".

Then, Willie Said Back To Kate "I Know Right, It's Being Cold of the Real Side of the Mist".

Then, Kate and Willie Went To The Kitchen To Get Some Food For Dinner as of Tonight's Deal, Angus and Lynn Kept Watching Cartoons as They Looked After The TV.

Lucky Had No Idea That He Didn't Get a Choice of Better Sitting on The Furnitures.

Next Day, The Dinner Night of Coming of All, Angus Monster Began To Have Dinner Jokes, He Said "I Wanna Why That I Eat Cats from The Planet, So I Was There and You Are There", Then He Laughed as of Yet for Funny Joke During The Family Dinner.

Sometimes, Lynn Said To Angus Monster "I Know How Did You Watched on TV When I Was There But By The Way, I Am Hungry".

So, The Tanner Family and Angus Monster Were Still Eating The Dinner For The Night of Life, But Kate and Willie Laughed at Them, So Angus Needed To Tell Jokes About Cats.

Angus Said "I Know For Spending Time Eating Cats and The Big Cats from The Best Planet. We Know How I Eat Cats from There" He Let Out a Specious Laugh at The Tanner Family Again.

"I Knew How I Eat All The Cats from The Other Places, So How Am I Doing For This Place To Eat". Then, Lynn Said "I Wonder Known How It is a Simple Appetite From Meaning the Word Bon Melmacian Diner, Huh, Okay".

Possibly, Lucky Gotten To The Smell of His Own Dinner. Angus Monster Said To Lucky "I Think Your Dinner is Ready".

Angus Sniffed Gently To His Nose Against Lucky's Food, The Smell Possibly Came Out of the Sensitive Time.

Willie Asked "What's That Smell?".

Lynn Answered "The Cat Food Sense of Smell".

So, Angus Monster Waved at Lynn's Waving Act, Kate Can Be Afford For Dinner Jokes as of Yet "I Need Some Help About This Joke For Two Times as I Say.... Okay Nothing Just a Bit Nothing at All".

So, Angus Monster and The Tanners Continue To Eat Dinner as Lucky Went To Eat Cat Food For The Rest of a Night.

Even The Night is Been Rested For Several Hours a Day, Lynn Had Enough of Dreaming For Cats.

In Before 1979 as Later at The Abandoned Farm Filled With Mist and Deadly Sources, Willie Tanner Walked Forward as He is Thinking of the Death Parasites.

Willie Shouted "Hello!".

He Got Into Beforehand Brave, Seeing a Bunch of Dead Horse In The Farm That Who Died of Exhaustion, Willie Had Gasped For Breath.

Willie Tanner Eventually Shouted Again "Is Everyone There!?".

Suddenly, He Found Out That The Red Deer Got Poisoned and Died From Eating A Chocolate, He Also Gasped To The Fierce.

He Walked Back To See That Happened, "Hello! Hello!! HELLO!!!" He Shouted.

He Saw The Dead Mother Wild Cat and The Wild Kittens That Died from The Infection, Willie Growled In Agony as He Didn't Get The Signs of Community.

Willie Groaned "I Missed That The Community Between Me and My Wife!", Then, He Ran Back To The House as He Got Into The Bad Days of Weekends.

Chapter 6: The Conical Free

Now in 1979, Before Brian Was Born.

The Hunter Suddenly Walked Up The Abandoned Park That He Announced That The Shooting Animals Will Be Soon In July of 1980.

The Hunter Said "The Shooting Animals Starts In July 7th 1980".

His Assistant Arrived For a Second, He Said "I Know What's You Been Thinking About It".

The Hunter Said "I Cannot Afford For Paying To That Mess".

The Hunter Ran Off To The Pay of The Shopping Spree, The Assistant Said "I Wonder Why He's Doing It".

He Walked Away To The Something Terrorized By The Shines of The Sun.

In June 1980, The Tanners Saw Angus Monster Chasing Lucky The Cat, He Said "Here Kitty Kitty Kitty".

Toddler Brian Looked Up, Lucky Gotten Into The Chair In The Living Room, Angus Monster Got a Great Townley Against His Way With Kate, Lynn and Willie.

Angus Monster Said "What Are We There With The Community Everyone".

Lynn Nodded Her Head "We Are Going to The Woodland Park, Mr. Monster".

Willie Grabbed The Bag and Said "We Are Going Now".

Then, Kate Alerted That The Hunter Closed Their Park "I'm Sorry, The Park is Closed Because The Hunter Began To Hunt The Animals".

Lynn Cried "Were Doomed, Kate, Were So Doomed".

Kate Apologizes To Lynn "I'm So Sorry Lynn, The Park is Sadly Closed".

Angus Nodded "Looks That Way".

Angus Monster Touched His Furry Chest Immediately as He Yawned Loudly In The Tired Way.

In Early August 1980, When The Animal Hunting Still Begin, Wallace, Madia and Daniel Hagen and His Dog Went Hiking In Their Long Journey.

Daniel Said "I Wonder What I Knew That The Dog is Walking".
So, The Golden Retriever Looked After The Hunter With The Poison Gun Which is Different, He Didn't Know For Those.

Wallace Said To Daniel "Don't Runaway My Dog, Mister".

But The Retriever Dog Ran Away To The Hunter, Madia Gasped from Her Breath, The Gunshot is Heard as The Dog Got Poisoned and Then, Dies as Well.

Wallace Gasped For Breath Eventually, He Cried "No! My Dog!".

Then, They Ran To The Dead Dog That Appear On The Ground, Wallace Cried Loudly as Daniel and Madia Watched.

Madia Cried as She Went "My Poor Doggie!".

It Happened Before, Daniel Groaned "I Will Never See My Dog Again".

Sometimes, Wallace, Daniel and Madia Picked Up The Dead Dog To Bury Him Back To The House.

Later in April 1981, The Toddler Brian Tanner Was Usually Playing But So, Lynn and Angus Monster Brought Up To Their New Lives.

Lynn Said "I Know My Arm is Almost Twisted".

Angus Monster Heard Something Terrible "Oh No! That's Not Good".

So, Willie and Kate Knew That Their Son is Here.

Kate Tanner Said "Look At My Sweet Son Brian".

"My Sweet Child" Said Willie Tanner.

So, Lucky Saw a Fly Flying Around In The Room, But Angus Monster Sees and Has To Chase Lucky from The Distance Shortly.

Lucky's Yowl Was Heard, Lynn Looked After Him, She Has To Call The Hagens That They Wanted To Rescue His Another Dog From Being Stuck In the Tent.

Lynn Said To The Phone "Hello, Hagens. Wallace's New Dog Got Stuck In The Tent, We Will Have To Rescue Him. Bye".

Then, Willie Got Outside.

Willie Spoke Up "Hello, Grenadine".

He Saw Angus' Grandson Named Grenadine Which He is a Other Brown Melmacian-Like Fox Alien.

Grenadine Said "Hi, Willie".

He Reviewed and Greet Angus Monster.

Angus Monster Spoke To Grenadine "Hello, Grenadine, How's It Going?".

His Sensational Sensitive Way as He Smiled, Lynn Met Grenadine as They Got Quick.

Lynn Just Sees Grenadine's Living Lives.

Lynn Spoke To Grenadine "Hi Grenadine, How Did You Got Here By Then, Are You Okay?".

Grenadine Said "I'm Good as Well, Lynn. How Far Can I See Me When I Was Here".

So, Kate and Willie Waved at Grenadine's Waving Life.

Grenadine Said "Hello, Kate and Willie".

Willie Said To Grenadine "Hello, Grenadine".

Kate Speaks Over To Grenadine Uniquely "Hi Grenadine, How Are You Doing?".

Grenadine Nodded and Said "Good, I Have An Idea About Myself Being an Undercover for the Park Unfortunately".

Supposedly, Lucky was Never Wanted To Be Melmacian Friend.

Grenadine Said and Asked To Lucky "Hello Lucky, What Are You Doing Here?". Lucky Knows

Grenadine Saw Him Immediately Which It Happened.

Later In October 1981, The Tanners Red The Book Against Angus Monster's Kindness.

Lynn Said To The Book "When all was quite ready, the Badger took a dark lantern in one paw, grasped his great stick with the other, and said, "Now then, follow me! Mole first, 'cos I'm very pleased with him;

Rat next; Toad last. And look here, Toady! Don't you chatter so much as usual, or you'll be sent back, as sure as fate!" The Toad was so anxious not to be left out that he took up the inferior position assigned to him without a murmur, and the animals set off ".

So, Angus Monster Loved The Wind In The Willows But He Chased Lucky Again Eventually from The

Couch to The Kitchen, Lucky's Yowl was Heard with Angus' Saying The Line "Here Kitty Kitty Kitty Kitty!".

Brian Saw Angus' Great Chase.

Lynn Said "I Gotta Get Out of Here", She Jumped off the Room To Get Lucky Immediately, and Then,

Lucky was Asleep Afterwards, Angus Monster Was Been Asleep Too in His Pet Bed

Chapter 7: The Abandon

In Early 1982, Brian is Now a 2 Years Old, Lynn Knew How Brian's Age is After The 1981 Birthday for The Tribute.

Lynn Said "My Thought is... I Am The Daughter of Kate and Willie, See! I Am Here".

and She Saw Angus Monster Controlling To Take Lucky Away, Lynn Gasped as She Has To Lose Lucky, She Has To Chase Angus Monster off the Control.

Lynn Yelled To Angus Monster "Hey! Come Back Here!".

Then, Angus Monster Has Still Picked Lucky Up, He Opened The Door Out of the Tanner's House, Rushing Off The Front Yard Into The Abandoned Woodland Park and They had Disappeared.

Lynn Cried Over The Disappearance of Angus Monster and Lucky Tanner.

Lynn Cried "My Poor Cat!".

So, Willie, Kate and She Told That Angus Monster is Missing.

Willie Said "Don't Worry Lynn, We Need To Call Everybody To Find Angus Monster and Lucky Who Got Lost In The Abandoned Woodland Park To Find Them".

Kate Said To Willie "Yeah Too, Willie. We Want To Find Angus Monster and My Cat Lucky Which They're Missing For Today".

So Kate, Lynn and Willie Possibly Walked To The Van and Then, Willie Drove Off To The Abandoned Woodland Park For Taking Too Long for Some Streets By Stopping For Restaurants, Gym, Pizza Place, Odd Old Farm, The Ochmonek's House and Many Other Streets That Are Finding On Their Way.

in Later October 1982, Angus Monster Got Lost, He is Looking for Cats to Eat. Angus Monster Said "I Am Trying To Look For Some Cats, Lucky".

He Worried That Lucky Tanner Got Stayed In The Empty Den, But First His Nose Snuffed Up Again as

He Sniffed His Scent of the Cat and Tasted a Smell of the Feline.

Angus Monster Said Again "I Am Ready To Find It For All of Us". and He Ran Across The Plan To Defeat The Hunter Immediately.

Suddenly on the Road for Pizza Place, Willie Said "We Are All Going To Eat Pizza Before We Find Lucky".

So, Lynn Thinks of the Smell, It Was a Pizza.

As Soon In September 3rd 1983, The Tanners Walked To The Forest To Find Lucky Tanner Being Lost.
Kate Shouted "Lucky!".
Willie Also Shouted Like Kate Does "Lucky Where Are You!?!" He Didn't Notice About After All "Lucky!".

Lynn Still Shouted as Willie's Disguise "Lucky!". So, Angus Monster Saw The Hunter's Home.

Angus Said "I See That Dog and The Cat Over There".

Then, He Sees a Pitbull Staring at Lucky Tanner, Pitbull Growled at Him Yowling Himself.
Lynn Yelled "It's Lucky!".

So, The Pitbull Dog Growled at Lynn Tanner's Angry Face, Lucky Hissed at The Dog, Smacked Him.

Angus Monster Growled "I Will Catch Lucky of Outta Here!".

Then, He Got In and Chase Lucky Once Again.

Lynn Growled After The Chase "Lucky, Please Come Back!".

So, The Hunter and His Assistant Arrived at Their Home But They Heard Lucky's Yowls, Meows and Hisses.

The Hunter Asked "What The Heck is That Noise, Mister?!".

His Assistant Answered "It Was Lucky Tanner. He is Meowing, Hissing, He's Screaming and Yowling".

So, The Hunter Heard Angus Monster's Catchphrase.

Angus Said To Lucky In The Chase "Here Kitty Kitty Kitty! Here Kitty Kitty!".

Then, The Hunter Grabbed His Gun Which He Can Shoot His Pet Pitbull Dog.
He Yelled "Dog!".

But He Accidentally Shoot Angus Monster from Mistaken as for Eating Cats, The Tanners Heard The Angus' Screaming Which He Got Shot and Injured by Him.

Lynn Cried "NOOOOOOOO!!!!!!".

So, Lucky Got Out of The Hunter's House, He is Found. Willie Said "Oh No, He's Got The Wrong Dog".

Then, Lynn Saw That Was Shocked About Him Being Shot and Wounded, She Had Been Sad For Now On, Kate Heard The Tragedy Accident.

The Hunter Said "Oh No, I'm So Sorry For Shooting The Alien Melmacian At All". His Assistant Said To Him "It's Okay, You Will Shoot The Dog".

Willie Popped Out of the Situation, He Groaned a Bit While He Itched His Arm. He Said "I Know Right, You Just Killed Your Wrong Dog".

So, Probably Lynn Tanner Was Thinking After Her Dad.

Lynn Tanner Cried "I Knew It, It Was Very Sad To Be The Announcement That He is Gonna Die Soon".

Kate Said To Lynn "It'll Be Okay, Daughter. You Will Live Without Him". So, Kate Hugged Lynn's Life.

And Then, Kate Finally Found Lucky Tanner from Their Way Home. Kate Cried "Lucky! I Missed You So Much That You're Alive".

Lucky's Reunion is Been a Bit Done For His Life.

Willie Said "I Was So Proud That Lucky's Reunion Was So Very Impressed".

Lynn Believed That Lucky Has Been Reunited With The Family, Lucky Was Very Happy and Safe. The Hunter's Assistant Told To The Hunter "So, You Killed Off That Angus Monster from His Great Chase".

The Hunter Said "I Believe So".

So, Angus Monster Was Still Moving To Be Picked Up By The Tanners, Putting Him In The Back of the Van.

And So, The Tanners Are Now on Their Way Home to See 2 Year Old Brian Tanner, They Know That Who Can To Find Lucky In There.

Finally, The Hunter Usually Shoots His Pet Pitbull With His Gun as The Dog was Yelp From The Death Resistance.

The Hunter and His Assistant Became a Hero Which They're No Longer an Enemy for The Tanners Which They Have To Open the Woodland Park Which They Have Something Knew For Their Chance.

Chapter 8: Sad News

Meanwhile This Evening In September 1983, Lynn and Willie Put Angus Monster Down To The Front Yard Which They Found Out He is Dying Which After He Just Crawled His Way Home.

Lynn Sadly Comments "I Know, I Think He's Dying!".

Willie Cried Over "I Know Right. He is Started To Die For Slowly Minutes".

So, Angus Monster Purely Groaned Out of His Injuries as Soon He Wants To Wait For His Death, He is Breathing by His Own Breath of His Mouth.

Angus Said For His One More Words "I Promised To You Lynn, I Was All My Preceded To Me. Please Help Me".

So, Willie Said To Angus Monster "I Was Wondering Angus, I Was Here In My Town of Los Angeles, California".

Angus Monster Said For His Last Words "I Knew It Could Be, Willie. No Ones Hurting Me for Some Reason Which is Why I Am.... An Alien".

So, He Fell Fast Asleep as He is Slowly Dying.

Willie Said To Said "I Know, I Was Very Thinking That He is Passing Away from Many Causes".

Lynn Said To Willie "I Know Willie, I Was Sad About It Happened That He is Slowly Dying".

Willie Standardly Said To Lynn Tanner "I Notice That They're Having a Sad News For The Family". Suddenly, Lynn and Willie Walked Back To The House as Kate and Brian was Sharing The Stuff For Something's Dinner.

Lynn Knows That Kate is Already Sad But Lucky is Just Standing On The Dinner Table From The Dining Room.

Kate Said "Lynn, It's Time For Dinner".

Lynn Said To Kate "Yes, Mom".

Then, Lynn Walked To The Dinner Table To Sit Down.

Later Then, The Tanners Found Out That Angus Monster Had Passed Away In His Sleep. Willie Cried Over His Dead Body "Oh No! My Poor Angus Old Monster!".

So, He Sobbed All Over The Place, Lynn Was Very Upset About Him.

Lynn Cried "Oh No! What Happened To My Angus Monster?!" She Has To Cry Immediately "My Poor Baby!".
So, Lynn Mourned Over His Dead Body as Her Family Sobbed as They Mourned Together.

Which is Before The Burial, Willie and Kate Was Very Upset Too.

Willie Sadly Said To Kate "We Will Have To Bury Him Tomorrow This Afternoon".

Kate Said To Willie's Sad Expression "Yes We Will, Willie, We Will".

Kate Comforted Willie Tanner For The Sudden Encounter.

Later This Afternoon, Willie Dug Out The Grass as Brian and Lynn Watched, Willie Asked To The Children "Ready, Kids?"

Lynn and Brian Answered "Yes".

and So, Angus Monster Was Put Down on The Dirt and is Now Buried Which The Tanners Dug Up The Burial Memorial as His Grave Was Added in The Backyard.

Kate Walked Up To See Willie Burying Lynn's Best Friend.

Kate Sadly Said "I Know Honey, I Know".

Willie Said To The Angus' Dead Body Which Was Buried "Goodbye, Son". So, He Completed The Burial.

Lynn Cried Over Angus' Grave "We Will Missed You, Sweetie".

So, Willie, Brian, Kate and Lynn Mourned Over The Death of Angus Monster Which He Died Yesterday of Evening as It's September 1983.

Epilogue

So, The Horse Carriage Arrives With The Hagens Always Have To His New Horse Named Harry II.

Wallace Asked To The Tanners "What Happened Here?".

Willie Answered Sadly "My Poor Guy Angus Monster Used To Be A Troublesome, He Eats Cats, He Befriends With My Daughter Lynn, He Goes on The Adventures and He Loves To Listen and Watching Television, So He is No Longer a Sweet Big Boy!".

Willie Sobbed Loudly.

Kate Said "It's Okay Willie, In September 12 to 13 of 1986, We Will Get a New Pet For Sooner as My Son Will Be Six Years Old".

Willie Said To Kate "Sure That We Will Get Another One".

Madia Said To Willie "Of Course You Do, Willie".

Daniel Said To Madia "Yes We Will Until 1986".

Wallace Cheered For Madia and Daniel Hagen for the Life "I Knew It, We Will Go To The New Farm With Us!".

So Kate, Willie, Lynn and Brian Has To Lead To The Backseat of the Horse Carriage, Possibly Without Angus Monster Which He Passed Away of The Early Evening.

The Horse Carriage Where Wallace, Madia and Daniel Hagen Knows as They All Leave The House To Go To The New Farm as They Decided To Go For a New Journey.

as of Yet In September 10th 1986, The Tanners Were Left Behind With The Hagen Family as They Always Met Their Match Before the Continue for The Long Journey Before The 12th of September.

The Tanner's New Alien Pet

Prologue

Once Upon a Time, It is September 10th 1986, The Adventure Just Continues as Brian, Kate, Lynn, Willie, Daniel, Madia and Wallace Living In The New Farm Followed By The Tanner's House.

The Following of The New Dog Named Bagels Who is Eating a Cooked Steak, Lynn Said "I Wanted To Eat a Pizza So Bad".

Willie Said "Me Too".

So, Kate and Brian Prepared For The Farewell For Tomorrow.

Kate Said "The Preparation Is.... We Are Gonna Leave a New Farm For Tomorrow Because of This Last Day of The Adventure".

So, Brian Tanner Waved At Daniel Hagen, Daniel is a Supervisor Farmer of the History and He has a Cool Outfit.

Lash Arrives When He Loved Lynn, How Daniel Nearly Should Say To Lash.

Lash Said To Lynn "I Want To Eat Too".

Lynn Said To Lash "Okay, Lash. Here We Go To Eat Pizza".

So, Kate and Madia Went On The Help.

Kate Said "We Help To Find Their Way Out".

Madia Coughed Up, She Set Off Her Typically To Her Husband.

Wallace Needed Helpings To His Wife Also.

Madia Said "I Know, Wallace. That's How When I Got There".

Lash and Lynn Went In For The Dinner, Daniel Had a Purpose For Snacked Down.

Lash Said "I Know... Pizza is Still Cooking".

So, Daniel Hit His Mother Madia In The Arm.

Madia Said "Oops, I'm Sorry".

Brian Immediately Thinks For Daniel.

Daniel Didn't Have No Idea How He Did.

Daniel Said "I Hope You Should Help Out The Business".

Madia Nodded "I Hope So, Daniel. We Will".

So, Lash and Lynn Were Together In The Action.

So, Kate Had No Idea with Willie Which They Are.

The Tanners Were Taking a Rest With The Hagens.

But Lash and Lynn Went To Eat Pizza After The Cooking Was Done.

Lash Said To Lynn "I Know That Pizza is Good".

Lynn Said Back To Lash "Yeah, Lash. It's Good".

So, Willie and Wallace Walked Towards The Garden But Seeing Other Corn Fields Being Filled With Watermelons.

So, The Riverbank Trials Began Towards Lynn and Lash's True Love.

So, Lynn Leads Lash For The Last Day of Week of Riverbank Day 1, They Got Into The Old Boat, Which Lynn Has Her Oar Which Appeared On Her Old Boat.

Lash's Feeling Had Never Helped With Sadness, But The Boat Rows Which Acclimated By Lynn's Oar.

The Boat's Row Started To Ride To The Riverbank's Rivers and Streams.

The River's Ditty:

"The river waits for you.
The river waits for anyone.
The river's running through
The lives of all of us.
It doesn't take a view.
It thinks the same of everyone.
And we should think that too,
The great and small of us.
So the story goes
As the river flows,
And the power of the story carries on and on and on and on and on.
Yes, the power of the story carries on and on and on and on and on."

So In September 12th 1986, Lynn was Glad to Go Here With Lash, So The Hagens Lead Willie, Kate, Brian and Lynn Back To The House.

Chapter 1: Dinner Confession

So Trustily, Daniel, Madia and Wallace Said To Goodbye To The Tanners, Doubly Notice For Horse Carriage When Leaved Off The Building.

Lynn Said "So, It Happened Here, Willie".

So Later At The Tanner's Kitchen, Kate and Lynn Are Making Dinner, Brian is Ahead of Craving But, Willie Picked Brian Up.

Willie Said To Brian "Okay Brian, Time To Eat".

Willie Knows To Put Brian On The Left Dining Chair, So Kate and Lynn Continued To Do.....

Peacefully as Mashed Potatoes and Salad Was Almost Finish Where Kate and Her Daughter Lynn, Typically Almost There To Something.

Willie Got Brian a Mashed Potatoes, Not To Mention That Willie Has a Meatloaf Which He Had Finished.

Willie Said "Okay Kate, How is That Possible When I'm Here But I Am".

Kate Said To Willie "Willie, I Need Help But I'm Almost Finished Making Food. But, Brian, Try Some Mashed Potatoes".

Brian Said To Kate "I Was Hoping You Say No".

Kate Knows Brian "Just Try More of Those and See What You Liked It".

Willie Finally Walked With His Silverware and Just Sits Down "Just Try a Little Bit, And Here Comes! Mister Meatloaf".

So, Kate Has To Sit Down as She Finished Her Dinner, Also Lynn Finished Her Food Too, Started Walking To The Chair During The Dialogue.

So, Kate Said "So The Dinner is Done Already"

Brian Said To Kate "I Don't Know What's All of That, Kate".

So, Lynn Walked and Just Sits On The Left Chair Next To Brian.

Puts Down the Salad for Anything, Wanted To Eat For Dinner For The Beginning.

So Correctly..... Lynn Said "How About Lash, He is Only 14 Years Old".

Sometimes Willie Said To Lynn "I Know How Lash is.... He is 14 Years Old Against Your 16 Years Old".

Kate Said "I Know Right".

Brian Flickered His Eyes and Said "I'm Worried from Those Mashed Potatoes".

Willie Said "You Don't Like Mister Meatloaf Either".

Sometimes Brian Walked Off To Pick Lucky The Cat Up To See Lynn.

But Lynn Tanner Said "Something Has Gotten Into The Great Beech of Lifting" She Always Spoke To Her Young Brother Brian "So, I Was Speaking To My Mom and Dad But I Was Not Own By Us, It Was The Sound of the Universe Eventually But Okay".

So, Brian Said "I Know That Lucky is a Good Cat".

Sometimes, Brian Put Lucky Down and Walked Fast Into The Couch.

Willie Said "What When We Suggest Us Now But I Said That I Was Kind".

Kate Always Said To Willie "I Notice That".

So, Lynn Got Up, Ran To The Bedroom To Get Something Else, Brian, Willie and Kate Are Spoke Up In The Kitchen.

Kate Said "So Willie, What Are We Suggestively For Doing Something For Now On".
Willie Said "I Was Notice For Us But Nothing..... Just Dinnertime".

Brian Said "But Dad, It's Not Just a Real Slight of Lucky But Just a Cat".

So, Kate, Willie and Brian Are Noticed That They Spoke Up To Go To Garage.

Chapter 2: The New Alien Pet

So, Willie and Brian Walked Outside To The Garage, So He Hold Brian's Hand To Walk Safe.

Willie Said "Brian, We Are Gonna See What The Garage is".

So, Brian Said "Willie, This is Entertaining Look".

Willie Said To Brian "I Know Just in Case It Got Bransom Ways To Look".

They Walked and Entered The Garage as They Turn The Lights On, Just To Take a Look At The Garage Room.

Brian Said "Wow, Look At The Garage" He Smiled Eventually "Pretty Neat".

So, Willie and Brian Walked Inside The Garage, But Anytime They Take a Look at The Garage Stuff Like Trains, Telescope, The Great Caller from The Space-Life and Many More.

So Willie Said "Look at Those Stuff, It Has Shortwave Radio Stuff, Telescope and Many More Stuff".

The Garage Door Has Wide Open Which Lucky Got Out of It Before Lynn Gets Him Again But Willie Spoke To Brian.
Willie Said "I Knew That Telescope is Gonna Be Accompanied, Brian".

So, Brian Walked Up To The Telescope as He Speaks To This "So, A Telescope is Known for The Stars But There is a Problem With Here...... But It Happened".

So, Willie Had Found a Shortwave Radio Speaker "Hello, Something Get Anything of Those Questions".

So, Lynn Arrived By Picking Her Cat Lucky Up, So She And Willie Thought of Something Without Any Questions.

Lynn Said "Yesterday, There's My Boyfriend Named Lash".

Willie Asked "What's Your Boyfriend's Name?"

Lynn Answered "Lash, He's Just 14 Years Old".

Willie Said "I'm Notice For Nothing Come Around In Here But Nothing is Perfect At All".

Since, Kate Arrived Over To Brian's Lives But Lynn Said "Okay, My Dad Hates Lash".

So, Kate Believed Brian "Okay Brian, Remember How It Happened Here" So She Thinks of Something Else "I Really Want To Say.... It is an Important Happening Here Between Everyone and Their Family Out Here But There's No Way To Get There".

Brian Said To Kate "Who Knows Us About Trying To Go Anywhere".

So, Kate Walked Up the Curtain To Close Down The Way of the Windows, She Said "I Know Right".

Brian Said "Who Else Joins In and Get Into Nighttime Path".

Kate Said "So, Go To Somewhere Else With Your Sister".

Brian Said "Okay".

So, Brian and Lynn Walked Out The Garage and Then, Kate Walked To Willie Who Knowing For Shortwave Radio Packed Up.

Kate Said To Her Husband Willie "So, I Notice Who Shortwave Radio Noticed from Someone Else".

Willie Said "Who Cares Who Noticed of My Shortwave Radio Is..... Not at All Such as Aroma and Food".

Kate Said "I Know Right, Who is Probably Thinking of Yugoslavia Is....."

Willie Never Thought It Was But He Gets To Continue To Call On His Shortwave Radio.

He Said "Kate, Who Never Thought It Was Yugoslavia's Thinks".

Kate Said "Followed With a Great Beeches Morning Nights".
Willie Shouted To His Wife Kate "Someone Who Called Nebojŝa!".

Sometimes, They Hear Nebojŝa's Speech Through On The Shortwave Radio's Speaker.

Willie Said "Who Notice My Thoughts of Who Are The Heroes Thinks".

Kate Said To Willie "So, I Heard Something Speaking as Well But Their We Are It Is".

Willie Said "Who Tell The Shortwave Radio's Nebojŝa Calls and I Think They Are".

Kate Said "Was Anything That Happened Before It's Too Late".

Willie Turned His Head Around and Said "Kate, Who Just Purpose To Other Staff".

Willie Tanner Has To Do Something With Calling On Shortwave Radio But He Thought of The Mistake That He Is.

The Flashing Lights Came From Spaceship With The Strange Creature.

Willie Said "They're Coming Up With The Lights Flashing" He Turned His Head Around Along With Kate "It's Coming".

He Stands Up Out of The Chair "It's Flashing, It's Happening in Here".

The Lights of The Garage Began To Turned Off, Willie Ran To Something That Goes Here, Looked Up In the Darkness.

He Said "That is Coming Up Something Else or What".

Then, Brian and Lynn Opened The Door and Ran To Their Parents.

Brian Said "The Lights, What Happened To The Lights".

Lynn Said To Brian "It is Coming".

Willie Said "I Think It Is".

As He, Kate, Brian and Lynn Ran Out The Door and Then, They Scared and Probably Heard The Crashing Sound Which Crashed Into the Roof.

The Smokes Probably Came Off from Spaceship, The Tanners Thinks They Are Something is Happening.

They Looked Up The Spaceship's Window, It is a Strange Creature Going On.

Willie Said "We Have a Visitor".

So, A Strange Creature Suddenly Thought of the Spaceship Window Being Hit In.

Chapter 3: Who Named ALF?

So, Lynn and Willie Carried The Blanket With Even a Strange Brown Creature That It Is, Probably Kate and Brian Thought They Are.

Brian Shouted "It's Hairy, It's Heavy, It's Furry!".

So, Kate Said "Yes, Brian, Look Here".

Lynn and Willie Wanted To Put The Strange Creature Down The Coffee Table But Lynn Said "No, Not The Couch But The Coffee Table".

So, Lynn Got To The Coffee Table To Pick Up Some Stuff Out and Put Down The Couch, Willie Puts The Brown Blanket That Had Strange Creature Down Into The Coffee Table.

They Turned Out To Be A Male Melmacian, as Kate and Brian Looked After.

Willie Has Looked at The Creature Sleeping, Who Knows Willie is Getting Down The Knees To Look Down At.

Sometimes, The Male Creature is Still Sleeping.
So, Brian, Lynn and Kate Were Shocked, Suddenly Brian Said "A Real Alien".

Kate Then Said "I Really Think It Is".

Willie Said "I Don't Know, Brian's Right It's An ALF".

Kate Asked "What?"

Willie Said "An ALF, Uh... A. L. F. That Short For Alien Life Form"

Brian Asked "Can ALF Stay In My Room?"

Kate Said "No, No This Thing is Not Stay In Anyone's It's Not Staying".

Brian Asked "Why Not? E.T. Got To Stay".

Kate Said "E.T. Was a Movie, This is Real" Who Thought "This is On Our Coffee Table".

Willie Then Said "This is Incredible, Truly Amazing" He Stands Up "After all those years of wondering, and hoping That it might be possible to contact alien life" He Thinks of It "To have this happen, it's a miracle. It's a Full of Lifelong Dream".

Kate Said To Willie "We Gotta Get Rid of It".

Willie Said "Absolutely. We don't know anything about it. It could be dangerous. It could be diseased. It could be hostile, Or have hostile friends or acquaintances. It could be anything"

So, ALF Began On His Dream From Dead-Brain About The Tanners Thinking from Him.

Lynn Asked "What if the authorities do something to it?"

Brian Asked Then Said "Yeah, what if they poke needles in it?"

Kate Answered "No, they wouldn't poke needles in it" Then Asked "Would they, willie?"

Willie Said "Well, they could, I don't think they would, but they could and They Might"

The Dream Ends With ALF's Wake-ness Without Anything To Do.

Kate Said "I Don't Know What They Are Exciting All About" She Said To Willie "Sometimes We Gotta Report This" Then Asked "Whatever Choice When It Is?"

ALF Got Up With Grunting But Then Asked "Ah? Can I Get a Suggestion?".

Willie Asked "They Are Sure Why Not?".

ALF Said "Well, if it's not too much trouble" Then, He Gets To Sit Up and Then Ask "How about fixing my spaceship?"

The Tanners Looked Shocked.

ALF Knows "Hello! Read my lips"

Kate Said "It Talks".

Brian Said "It's Hairy, It's Heavy and It Talks".

ALF Said "Good" Then Asked First "Now what about fixing my spaceship So i can get my heavy, hairy body out of here?"

Willie Said To ALF "i'm not sure I can fix your spaceship... i mean not tonight but in the dark".

ALF Said To Willie "You Could Use a Light of Driveway..."

Willie Said "You Know That It Happened...... Nothing's Gonna Happen To All".

Kate Replied "Willie!"

Willie Said "I'm Sorry About This, I Just Seem So Human".

ALF Said "Hey, there's no need for name calling".

Kate Said "I Don't Think It is Too Friendly for Us or All of That".

ALF Said "She's Right. Let's Have a Snack Now Then Will Get Friendly Later".

Willie and Kate Both Noticed "Snack? What kind of snack? You got a cat? You eat cats? You can't eat lucky. No cat eating. not in the house, First That Other Alien Chased Lucky When Tried To Eat Then Now You" as They Both Said To ALF.

ALF Then Said "How About a Cat Food Can" Probably Asked For is Enough.

Brian Asked "Can we give alf a can, mom? Please? Please?".

Kate Answered "Alright".

Lynn Said "Okay This is Too Much After The Hagens Said Goodbye To Me and My Family".

Willie Said "Yes It Is".

Lynn and Brian Walked To The Kitchen But ALF Gets Up and Follows.

Lynn Said "We're Going With You".

ALF Said "Trust Me About as Far as She Can Throw Me".

Willie Said "However They Follow Each Other Without Figuring It Out Behind".

Kate Said "How About Noticing Us at All, Willie".

Sometimes Willie Said "You Should Love Me as It Can".

So, Kate and Willie Tries To Kiss from The Distance But Lucky Jumped Off The Kitchen Window as ALF Tries To Chase Him, They Hear Lucky's Yowl.

ALF Said "He's Quick, I Will Give Him That".

So, ALF is Adopted by The Tanners as The New Alien Pet.

They're Happy.

Chapter 4: Bathroom Ristorante

So The Next Morning September 13th 1986, Kate and ALF Woke Up In Bed, Sometimes Kate Heard The Alarm Clock Buzzing Which It Is.

Then, She Turned It Off Immediately.

Kate Said "Morning".

ALF Said "Morning".

Then, Kate Wakes Up Screaming At ALF.

ALF Screams At Kate Back as Was Frighten.

Kate Screamed "Willie!"

ALF Screamed Back "Willie!".

Then, He Got Out of Bed and Ran To The Bathroom as The Door Shuts.

"What's Going On There?" Asked Willie.

ALF Said "Nothing.... Just Screaming".

Willie Ran The Door Open To The Bedroom as He Sees Kate.

Kate Said "Let Me Think of It, Willie" She Noticed To Willie "I Do Not Think This is Gonna Be a Workout".

Willie Said "I Will Take Care of It" He Meant To Be There To Run For Kate "Everything's Fine Everything's Under Control".

Then, He Kissed Kate With The Shaving Cream On The Face, He Wiped Off of the Kate's Face with The Towel.

Willie Heard The Toilet Flush, He Ran Towards The Bathroom, Closes The Door.

ALF Sees The Flushing of the Toilet.

Which ALF Said "Interesting Concept".

Willie Ran To Get ALF Over Here.

He Said "Come Now, Come On, Come On, Come On".

As ALF Walked To Willie Which was Around, "Over Here By Me" Said Willie as Over Again "We Have A Bit Trouble Over Here, to Discuss".

ALF Said "Yeah, Lynn and I Had Gathering Last Night. So I Promised Here" He Got Willie's Glasses On And Asked "Oh Boy You're Blind as a Bat Aren't You?".

Willie Asked To ALF "Could You Give Those To Me".

Willie Gave ALF From His Glasses Back "No Problem" Said ALF.

ALF Shook His Fur and His Head as He Didn't Think of Gathering, Willie Was Still Shaving.

"I Don't Know. Kate was Very Nervous About Whole Thing...." Said Willie.

"Absolutely" ALF Said As He Brushes His Fur, Then Asked "Who's Kate?"

Willie Said "No, ALF" He Took His Brush Back from His Hand.

"Oh Yeah, She's Snores" Said ALF.

"She Doesn't Snore" Willie Said.

"You're Calling Me a Liar?" Asked ALF.

"Just Keep Your Distance, Alright" Said Willie "And Try To Be Consider It Okay".

"No Problem" ALF Said and Then, He Sprayed The Shaving Cream On Willie.

"Give It Back To Me!" Exclaimed Willie as He Gets Shaving Cream Can Back To His Hand.

"Who Knows The Considers Absence! As Well for All!".

Willie Was Mad But Wanted To Be Finished Doing It "Let's Just Settle Down Here, Just Take a One Step At The Time".

He Grabbed The Razor Shaving Back as ALF Picks It Up.

Willie Said "There's No Need To Be Shaved, You'll Look Fine".

Then, ALF Asked "Well Everything You Do?" And Said "You're My Idol".

Willie Looked at ALF as Getting Precious of Thoughts, ALF Looks At Willie Back as He Gets Any of Cuteness.

"Umm...." Said Willie "I'm Gonna Take a Shower Now".

"Help Me In" ALF Said.

Willie Took a Towel On The Hanger And Said "I'd Love To Take Any of Long" Then He When Gets In Over Said "Thank You".

ALF Then Said "Okay, Just Do Not Use The Hot Water".

Willie Knows To Take His Blue Housecoat Off as He Gets To Shower, But ALF Looks At It, Willie Then Said "Just To Be In Mind".

ALF Probably Just as Saying "Never Saw a Thing".

He Knew That Happened But Willie Said When Holding His Housecoat "Then Stay Away from That Window There is a Nosy Neighbor Mrs. Ochmonek".

So, ALF Thought It Was But Said "Ochmonek... Sounds Like The Typo".

Willie Said "Just Don't Wanna See It, She Will Turn It In".

So, ALF Looked After But He Climbs Up, Knocking Those Soaps, Shampoos, Conditioners and Others Down Into The Floor, Sees Mrs. Ochmonek In The Window.

Raquel Said "The Red Fox is Just a Kidding Nosy Fox Around Here....." She Scratched Her Head Quickly.

Hearing a Fox's Bark, Raquel Looked at Something, But ALF Looks At Her.

Raquel Asked "Trevor, is This a Such Between a Kangaroo and The Aardvark?" She Noticed "I See a Fox But Never Saw It".

Trevor Said "Oh Stop Being Such a Crossbow Gaye...."

Raquel Said "I'm Not Talking About Anything, I See an Alien In The Window".

Trevor Asked "What?".

ALF Got Down, Ran Though The Red Towel Over In The Bathroom.

Trevor Said "I Don't See Anything".

Raquel Said "I Think It's Shaving or Something".

But ALF Got The Table and Wipes The Window Over The Conversion.

Raquel Gasped Into Her Lungs.

Then, ALF Ran To Get The Toilet Paper.

Willie Asked "Towel?".

ALF Asked Loudly "Are You Talking To Me!?".

Willie Said "Yes I'll Get These".

ALF Then Said "You Got It" Then He Rolled The Toilet Paper as He Gets Noticed.

Willie Walked And Sees ALF Holding a Toilet Paper Afterwards.

ALF Said "Less Than A Trick".

Willie Grabbed The Bunch of Toilet Paper, He Got Something.

"No Problem" Said Willie.

He Gets Wiped Off By Himself.

Chapter 5: The Garage Proud Mary

Once In The Garage, The Train Roves The Tracks, ALF Completely Wearing His Earphones.

ALF Than Sang:

"Left a good job in the city
Workin' for the man ev'ry night and day
And I never lost one minute of sleepin'
Worryin' 'bout the way things might have been
Big wheel keep on turnin'
Proud Mary keep on burnin'
Rollin', rollin', rollin' on the river"

Lynn Doesn't Notice But Willie Keeps Calling ALF's Name When He's Singing.

Lynn Doesn't Know Why, Hearing ALF's Yell "Yooowwll! Yeah!".
Then Asked "How Are You Up There Doing Will You?!".

Willie Said "I Can Use a Little Help, But No Information How It Is....".

ALF Said "How About a Key There And It Goes.....".

Willie Looked Down Sadly But Lynn Tried To Looked Up But She Walked.

Then Lynn Said "ALF, Maybe I'll Get The Wrench For My Dad..... My Speech is".

ALF Said "Hey Lynn, How Don't Have a Phone.... Do You...."

Lynn Said "No, How It Is..."

ALF Said "I Gotten a Bonus Tune" He Now Noticed "For a Now Porch, But I Was Nothing To Talk To Us".

ALF Knows a Phone Number While Lynn Ran To The Call But Willie Yelled Trough the Ladder By Rocking It.

ALF Continues To Finished The Phone Number, Then He Smiled Immediately After That.

Lynn Gave Willie a Mechanized Wrench as It Served a Word "Thank You".

"ALF, I Think You Can Make Our Contact" Said Lynn "People".

ALF Said By Sadly Commenting "I Have Tried.... I Tried Again and Again, It's an Exercising Failure. Uh.... I Lived Face It" Then, He Cried "I'm Trapped Here! I Will Never See The Purple Side of My Planet Again!".

ALF Cries The Temper Soberly Immediately But He Sadly Cries a Bit, Then He Moaned as His Head was Up.

Lynn Heard Something No Idea It Is.

"Too Dramatic" ALF Said.

"Oh ALF" Said Lynn But Asked "What Are We Gonna Do With You?".

ALF Said "I Guess You'll Loved Me as It Last".

Then, Lynn Hugged ALF as The Ditty Calls The Malcolm's Part.

The Original ALF and Lynn's Ditty:

"Big wheel keep on turnin'
Proud Mary keep on burnin'
Rollin', rollin', rollin' on the river
Rollin', rollin', rollin' on the river
If you come down to the river
Bet you gonna find some people who live
You don't have to worry 'cause you have if you got no money
People on the river are happy to give
Big wheel keep on turnin'
Proud Mary keep on burnin'
Rollin', rollin', rollin' on the river
Rollin', rollin', rollin' on the river
Rollin', rollin', rollin' on the river
Rollin', rollin', rollin' on the river
Rollin', rollin', rollin' on the river"

So, The Called Out Ditty Plays, Willie Knew The Ditty Is.

"The Ditty Has Came" Said Willie "How Is Perfect Listen".

ALF Walked Out of The Garage and He Said "Yo' Lucky My Man".

The Lucky's Meow was Heard Shortly After ALF Walked Off.

Chapter 6: Looney Tunes and Alien Task Force Man

Meanwhile, Brian and ALF Are Watching Bugs Bunny Marathon On TV Apparently as Kate was Busy.

Brian and ALF Noticed And Was Saying Anything:

"So, What Are Gonna Keep In Secrets" Said Brian.

"Who Cares, Who Knows It" Said ALF.

"Whoever That Knows Bugs Bunny Marathon" Said Brian.

The TV Heard As the pitcher, Bugs tells us, "Eh, I think I'll perplex him with my slowball."

The ball moves so slow, three Gorillas in a row can't hit it.
"One. Two. Three strikes, you're out. One. Two. Three strikes, you're out. One. Two. Three strikes, you're out."

"Oh, bat boy," calls Bugs.

A uniformed boy with bat wings flies to Bugs with bats to choose from.

Bugs hits the ball and runs the bases.

At home he unfurls a pinup poster to distract the catcher and score a run.

Another time he has such a heated, in-your-face argument with the umpire that he winds up inside the ump's face mask, chewing the ump's cigar.

He pulls the classic switch, tricking the umpire: "Out - safe - out - safe - out - out - safe - out - I say you're safe! If you don't like it, you can go to the showers!"

Bugs the catcher continues to cheer on Bugs the pitcher.

"Atta boy. That's the only pitchin' it. Come on. Right down the old alley!"

So, ALF and Brian Watched Baseball Bugs, ALF as When He Said "So, I Gotta Get Something To Drink".

Brian Said "Me Too".

They Got Up and Walked To The Kitchen, But Kate Stands Up and Asked "Where You Too Going?".

Brian Turned Around and Said "We Gotta Get Something To Drink".

ALF Said "We're Harsh".

Kate Said "Okay, but No soda pop, and nothing to eat before dinner".

"Yes M'am" ALF and Brian Both Said.

As They Walked To The Kitchen, Kate Sat Down Trying To Read The Wind In The Willows Book.

The Pop-Top Cans Opening was Heard as Kate Looks Shocked.

Brian and ALF Are Seen Holding a Beer, Kate Then Yelled "I Said No Soda Pop!".

Brian Said to Kate "That's Not Soda Pop That's Beer".

Then, ALF Burped and Now He Said "You're About Our Things Out of Coors".

Kate Got Up, Asked "What?" She Ran To ALF and Brian, Then Takes Two of Beers Away "Give Those To Me!".

ALF Said "Hey... Careful There is Still Full".

Kate Put Down Two Beers Into The TV Top, She Blamed At ALF.

"Now You Listen To Me ALF I Will Not Allowed This Over Behavior!" Yelled Kate "This Boy is Actually 6 Years Old is Not to Drink Beer and You're Not To Drink But Does, I Don't Know How Is This Happening To Us and All of That!".

"Melmac" Said ALF.

"What?" Asked Kate.

"Melmac" ALF Said "This is Name of My Planet".

Kate Asked "You Can't Go Back To Melmac?"

"It Exploded" ALF Said "It Mind Which This is My Street. Now, if willie fixes my ship, I suppose i could start a new life somewhere else On some desolate, crater-Filled asteroid, And spend the rest of my life fending off gamma rays"

"No, ALF No" Brian Cried "We want you to stay here with us, don't we, mom?"

Kate Then Said "Yes, How Kid Wants To Stay" Then Asked "ALF, Do You Get Your Own Mind?"

"No Problem" ALF Said.

Kate Said "But We can't hide alf forever, and i can't go on like this; Watching him every moment, Wondering what he's going to do next"

Then, She and Brian Heard The Burp Came from ALF, He Put The Beer Down Enough.

Kate Said "Maybe He Will Be Good".

Brian Said "I Saw Baseball Bugs as of This".

So, ALF Walked To The Couch and Said "What's Up From Distance".

Then, Lucky Walked as He Meows.

ALF Asked "How Are You Doing, Lucky?" He Looks Shocked from Something From The Distance "Cross My Heart!".

So, He Thought "See? No Problem", Then He Groaned as He Turned Around To Look Here, Brian and Kate Heard The Door Knocking.

"Oh No" Cried Brian "What Could That Be!?".

"I Don't Know" Said Kate

"Don't Answer It Mom, Please!" Cried Brian.

ALF Walked and Climbed Up The Window, Kate Said "Brian, I'm Going To Answer The Door".

"No" Cried Brian.

"Yes" Said Kate "It's Probably Mrs. Ochmonek Which She Is".

"It's Not Mrs. Ochmonek" ALF Said.

"What?" Kate Asked.

"This is Not Mrs. Ochmonek. Less It's Joining the Army" Said ALF.

He Gets Down Shortly, He Walked Away as Soon as He Can.

Kate Walked Up, Said To ALF "It is Task Force Man".

Kate Then Noticed Out, Brian Asked Sadly "What Would They Take ALF Away?!".

Kate Said "I Don't Know Brian, You Know What's Knowing To Do. Try This Understand Okay".

Brian Sadly Said "Yeah, Kate".

The Door Knocking Was Heard Again.

ALF Said "That Taken is Not Noticed".

Kate Ran To ALF But Willie and Lynn Came Up Walking Which It Is, Kate Asked "Did You Fix a Spaceship?".

"No, Kate" Said Willie "I'm Not Fixing This Spaceship Right Now".

The Door Knocked Over It Once Again.

"Kate, What Will Be" Said ALF.

So, Kate Opened The Door... It Was..... An Alien Task Force Man.

"Mrs. Tanner" Said The Task Force Man.

"Yes?" Asked Kate.

"I'm James McDowell" Said The Alien Task Force Man "I'm The Task Force Hero of The Distance".

He Won't Mind Here "May If I Come In?" He Asked.

"Yes, James" Kate Answered.

"Still Fine of All" Said The Alien Task Force Man "Well.... I Saw What Happened Here Between Someone and Sometimes.... Shouldn't Know for Space Creature".

"The Space Creature" Kate Said.

"Yes" Said The Alien Task Force Man "He's Hairy, He's Been An Hour of Course".

Kate Asked "Is He Consider a Distance or What?".

"Hard To Tell To Get In The Lab" The Alien Task Force Man Answered.

"And Sometimes, Whatever Did We Get Him In The Lab?" Asked Kate.

"Oh, the usual battery of tests" The Alien Task Force Said "We'll see how he responds to intense heat, Freezing cold, High voltage, Toxic substances, Pain, Sleep deprivation, Inoculation, That's needles, And of course, dissection".

Then, ALF Gulped as Was Heard By.

Kate Asked "Why Don't You Just... Pull the Toenails Out?".

"It Did Not Let Me Finished" Said The Alien Task Force Man "Who Cares".

So, Kate, Willie, Lynn and Brian Were Shocked.

Kate Said "Don't Bother. We Are Not harboring any space creatures".

So, "Fine" Said The Alien Force Man "Thank You".

Willie Asked "excuse me, sir, Could you tell us who gave you our name?"

"As i told mrs. Tanner, that information Is strictly ochmonek, uh, anonymous" Said The Alien Task Force Man "Good Bye".

So, James McDowell Walked Away as The Tanners Watched.

Willie Closed The Door Shut, "Thanks, Mom" Said Brian.

"Thanks, Mom" Lynn Said.

"Yeah" Said ALF "Thanks, Mom".

Then, He Hugged The Tanners By The Happiness.

"I Love This Woman" ALF Said.

As The Tanners Kept Hugging, ALF Hugged Again.

So Later at Night of The Garage, ALF Walked and Straight Over To Shortwave Radio, The Bold of Free as He Courage a Happiness Which He Takes Over The Angus Monster's Role.

The Bang was Heard With The Radio "The Melmac Touch" ALF Thought "Hello? Anybody there? Yo! Calling anybody from melmac" He Might Asked "Hello? Skip? Larry? Muffy? It's gordon".

The Tanners Walked To The Garage as They Saw ALF Calling On The Shortwave Radio.

"So, Look" Said ALF "That's What The Living Thing Who It Is... That's What They Called A Family".

So, ALF Was Thinking To Look Behind "So, There's a Guy Named Willie, There's His Wife Kate, They Got Good Heart as They Are, Okay, The Extract of Her Hair For Same Natural Color, Ha Ha Ha! They Got Two Kids Unfortunately, They Both Idolize Me".

So, Lynn and Brian Watched as ALF Continues To Call On The Shortwave Radio.

ALF Has Set To Call "So, They Are.... I Will Really Missed Y'all, So It Never Breaks My Heart For Something Again, Who Try To Get In Touch as The Introduced To Lovely People".

So, Lynn and Brian Wanted To See How It Happened, Brian Was Too Late To See Angus Monster Which He Died "You're Too Late" Said Lynn.

"I Know" Cried Brian.

Lynn Hugged Brian Immediately as He Sniffled and Cries.

"Don't Cry" Lynn Sadly Comments Brian "It'll Be Okay".

So, The Tanners Decided That ALF is a New Alien Pet.

So, They Decided For Something To Know.

Chapter 7: The So Called Dinner Joke

One Night, ALF and The Tanners Were Having Dinner, So Before Lynn Met Lash.

ALF Said "This is we could eat their cat! So, the droid says to the "cranble" To tell the truth, i'd feel better If she lived another way" He Laughed as The Tanners Giggled Immediately "Yeah The Dinner Jokes Are On Here Again".

So Kate Said "I Knew That Dinner Jokes Take The Roles of All, Since In 1978, Angus and I Used To Have a Dinner Jokes With My Daughter When She Was 8 But Angus Was No Longer a Sweet But Troublesome Anymore, Lynn is Now 16 Years Old".

Brian Said When He's Eating Mashed Potatoes "Now I Like Mashed Potatoes, Mom".

Kate Then Said "Thanks, Brian".

So, Willie Said "We Can Know How It Is".
Kate Said To Willie "I Know Right. It Was Just Something Else Which Was True".

Willie Said To Kate Back "Easy True But No One Says That Happened, We Use To Have The First Alien Monster Dog For a First Time But He Died And No Longer a Pet".

Kate Said "I Know Right, Just a Great Time For Dinner".

ALF Joked Around Like He Does "I wear a size 5, But nothing with feet in it!" Then He Laughed Again "Oh, i've got a zillion of them".

He Knows Before "We Know That You Didn't Like? So Conversation For All... These two space travelers are going through andromeda, And they run into a space patrol. He was a rookie".

Kate Said "That Joke is Funny" as The Tanners Laughed at ALF's Jokes.

Just Before They Eat Their Dinner as Well.

They're Just Happy of the All Time Where They Could.

ALF is Just An Sweet But Troublesome Alien as He Can, He is A Melmacian Raised Up From Against Spaceship.

Lucky Eats The Bowl of Cat Food as He Could For Smell of Something Else.

The Moon Lights Up The Sky from Distance.

Willie Said "What a Same Thing as They Do What Else".

Brian Said "I Know Right".

Lynn Said "Dinner Considers Me Too".

ALF Said About a Joke "Eating Cats, Sometimes Drool But Nothing" He Laughed at Something "No Cares About Me, But a Fine Joke What It Is".

Brian Said "It Was Only One Knowing My Sister is True".

Lynn Said To Brian "Life Wished But Nothing Just a Simple True To Jack's Hagen Farm".

Brian Said "Thanks To All of Us".

Willie Said "I Know Right, It's Still Dinner Time".

ALF Then Laughed and Said "Cats Are Just Perfect To Eat All of Them as Well But Maybe Three".

Kate Said "Whatever It Happened Now, ALF".

Willie Said "We Are Trying To Eat Dinner, Kate" So They Are Eating The Dinner Before Then. It Happened First After The New Adventures But They Are Perfect For Same.

Chapter 8: The ALF of Los Angeles

So In September 14th 1986 By The Next Morning, Lynn Walked Outside Formerly By Someone Else But Brian, Willie and Kate Were Gathered In Outside the World.

Brian Said "Hey Lynn".

Lynn Said "Hi, Brian".

Willie Said "Fun In The Day, Kate" He Trusted as It Tried To "It Can Be Repatriation The Way of Ourself".

Kate Said "I Know Right. It Was Good But Summer is Almost Over, Willie".

Willie Said "Yes, Kate" He Nodded His Head "It Is".

Brian Said "I Know Right".

Lynn Said "Yes, Brian It Is".

So, Happiness Cleared Out The Skies of the Blue Shyness, The Grasses Are Green and The Clouds Are White.

ALF Considered Walking Against Happiness Between The Tanners.

ALF Said "We Need You".

Lynn Said "ALF, Hello There".

So, ALF Said Back "I'm Good".

So Kate, Willie, Brian and Lynn Gathered a Group, Brian Knew It Happened, ALF Joined The Group of Happiness.

They Looked Happy as They Looked at The Clouds.

Willie Said "I Knew That Los Angeles, California is Good for The Family, Who Cared and Loved The Earth and The Part of the Family Group, Must of Happiness Indeed".

Brian Said "Yeah Dad, Just a Clouds In Part of the Family Now".

Lynn Said "Wow, The Clouds Are Perfect For The Outside".

Kate Said "Niceness Way To See Our Skies".

Willie Said "We Can See The Skies and All The Indeed Way".

ALF Said To Brian "I Knew It Was a Family".

Brian Said "Yes, ALF. It is A Family".

So, Lynn Smiled a Happiness Leads For Care, Loved, Sweet and Nice.

Lash Arrived in the Backyard as He Said "Hi Lynn".

Lynn Said "Hi, Lash" Then Asked "What's Up Over Here?"

Lash Answered "I Promised That The Hagen Family Left Me a Message from the Letter".

Lynn Said "I Knew It, Just Take a Look At The Letter".

So, They Looked at The Letter To See How The Hagen Family Wrote a Message from Lynn's New Boyfriend.

Lash Noticed "That's Pretty Cool".

Lynn Said "Yes, How It is Going to Be Possible".

Lash Asked "How Is It?"
Lynn Answered "ALF and I Went Promised from The Backyard".

Lash Said "I Know Right, It Was Very Possible To Say How It Happens Before I Came Here".

Lynn Replied "Lash, That's Very Nice".

So, Lash Hold Lynn's Hand from The New Adventure Encounter.

So, They're Happy About It.

Epilogue

So, Lash Said "Thanks, Lynn".

Lynn Than Said "You're Welcome, Lash".

So, Lynn and Lash Got From The Adventure Encounter's Begin Their Journey as Kate, Willie, Brian and ALF Waved At The Last Moment from The Distance.

Lynn and Lash Were Very Proud of The Hagen Family's Best Future Adventure from The Farm.

Once, Kate, Brian and Willie Will Never See Angus Monster Again, They Will See ALF's Life as They Knew It Happened.

Brian Said "It Was Possible, Willie, It Was Possible".

Willie Replied "Brian, That's Great. They Can See Their Lives".

ALF Then Said "No Problem. Willie's Got An Idea For That".

So, Brian Hugged ALF's Life from The Happiness from Ending Towards The Life.

www.ingramcontent.com/pod-product-compliance
Lightning Source LLC
Chambersburg PA
CBHW080754120626
46557CB00005B/1263